Timmy
and the Ten
Commandments

Luke Morris

ISBN: 9781707927562 (paperback)

Dedication

This book is for Grace Lynn, Ethan James, Arden Dee,
Kennedy Hope, Jaxon Taylor, Rilynn Ann, Dilon Matthew,
and my Maranatha Kids.

I pray that you know Jesus and love
Him with all that you are!

Acknowledgements
& Thanksgiving

*"Every good and perfect gift is from above, coming
down from the Father of the heavenly lights, who
does not change like shifting shadows. He chose
to give us birth through the word of truth, that we
might be a kind of first fruits of all he created."*
James 1:17-18

Anything good that is within these pages truly deserves to be attributed to God alone. May His good gift of truth and creativity bring Him glory. I am thankful beyond words that He has allowed me to be a vessel to carry and reflect these gifts to others.

He has given me such good gifts through the people in my life that have shaped, encouraged, challenged, and helped me in my personal life to know God, grow in Him, and be used for His purposes.

Dad and Momma, thank you for your humble hearts and for establishing a grace-filled home on the foundation of Jesus. Dad, you have reflected my heavenly Father's heart to me like no other man, and have been used to show me that when we choose to walk in the light, darkness has no power. Momma, your love for God, His Word, and for other people, is unmatched by anyone I know and inspires me to seek God and know Him better. Thank you both for being my biggest cheerleaders and for pointing me to the Father.

Stephanie, I am overwhelmed by God's goodness to allow me to have a big sister who cares about me so deeply. God has used you to give me confidence in Him in ways you will never know. Thank you for sacrificing time and talent to help me edit this book—I will always treasure our time spent working on this project.

Ryan, I could not ask for a better brother or best friend. Thank you for being a constant encouragement to me my entire life. Your humble, steadfast spirit brings so much encouragement to me. The way you live out your convictions under the Spirit's leading is a great example and encouragement to your little brother.

Michael and Emily, I couldn't be more thankful to have the gift of family extended through you two! My heart is so full of joy knowing you both are partnering with my siblings to point your children to the Savior of our souls.

Elizabeth Smith, God has used you in great ways to teach and disciple me. Thank you for being faithful to Him in all that you do.

Cody Kargus, thank you for allowing me to partner with you in shepherding Maranatha by using my gifts for God's glory. I will always treasure #MyRiceLakeAdventure.

Lynsee Schnacky, you are a treasured friend. Thank you for being an encouragement to me on my best and worst days and for listening to *Timmy* over and over again.

Stacey and Carmen, thank you for always being ready to listen to me and let me process the excitement of this project... and pretty much everything else in my life.

My Maranatha family, thank you for inviting me into your lives and allowing me to live out God's call as part of the local body. Thank you for encouraging me to put *Timmy* in a format that will last a long time. I love you more than you will ever know.

A Prayer For All Who Read This Book

May all who read these pages better know the heart of God. In His great love, He has given us the Ten Commandments so that we can see His wisdom and our need for Jesus. May we humbly remember we can't meet God's standard on our own, and find all we need in Jesus. May God's Spirit change our lives so that we love God and others better!

Meet the Taborskys

The small town of Spice Lake, located in Harron County, is a lot like any Midwest town in America.

It has cold, cold winters with beautiful snowfalls that cover the pine trees, making it look like a picture from a calendar.

Spice Lake also has beautiful, sunny summers. During this time of year, you won't drive past the lake of Spice Lake without seeing someone casting their fishing line or walk by the Green Pine River without spotting someone floating downstream in a kayak.

Yes, Spice Lake is a lovely town, and it is filled with many hardworking families.

One of these families is the Taborsky family. In the Taborsky family, there are five people.

First, there's Mr. Taborsky, the father, whose first name is Kyle. Mr. Taborsky is a welder and has been for about fifteen years. He leads his family well and is kind and patient with his kids, at least most of the time.

Then there's Mrs. Taborsky, the mother. Mrs. Taborsky's first name is Estelle. She works part-time at the elementary school as the school librarian. She is sweet and creative, always seeming to know what to say and how to say it.

The oldest Taborsky child is Johnathon. He just turned fifteen and is finishing his first year in high school. He is very athletic and is naturally good at every sport he tries.

The youngest Taborsky child is Rose Marie—a four-year-old with enough spunk for the entire Taborsky family, or rather the entire town of Spice Lake! And please, make no mistake to simply call her Rose, for she will quickly remind you that her name is Rose Marie, *not* just Rose (and if you really want to make her happy, you should call her "Princess Rose Marie").

Then there's Timmy, the middle Taborsky child. Timmy is a very smart kid who is younger than most of the other kids in his grade. He won't turn eight until late November but just finished the second grade. He is kind and thoughtful and usually willing to help others.

It is this very smart, kind, middle child that this story is mostly about. Timmy Taborsky is going to experience a very special summer, and all that he does and learns will be shared with you!

Chapter 1

The month of June is just beginning. School has less than a week left before Summer Break, and Timmy Taborsky has one thing on his mind: baseball.

Timmy has been in tee-ball the past three summers, but this year he is finally old enough to move up to the baseball team, the *real* baseball team, and he couldn't be more excited!

Timmy has been planning and preparing for his grand entrance into the sport of baseball ever since tee-ball last season.

His new team is the Spice Lake Salamanders. The Salamanders' team colors are gold and blue. So, for Timmy's birthday and Christmas gifts this past year, he made sure his mom knew he wanted all his gifts to be one of those two colors.

From his new winter hat to his brand new socks, he is always completely covered with the gold and blue of the Spice Lake Salamanders—every day in every season!

Not only does Timmy try to look like a Spice Lake Salamander, but he also wants to act like one.

This past spring, he didn't miss a Bruisers game on TV and went to each of the home baseball games for Spice Lake High School.

Timmy even looked up videos when his parents let him.

He would watch how different players would get ready for a game, soaking up all he could from their advice.

On the weekends, Timmy would beg his big brother, Johnathon, to play catch with him so he could work on his pitching.

Being part of the Spice Lake Salamanders is what got Timmy excited to wake up in the morning, and it's what made him go to bed when his parents said, for he had learned that sleep was very important for athletes.

Every night he placed his baseball glove on the table right by his bed so that it was the last thing he saw when the lights went out, and the first thing he saw when the sun peeked through his window the next morning.

Timmy is definitely devoted to baseball and to making sure he would have the best season possible. He was convinced that if he worked hard and stayed focused, he would be a great baseball player!

But, one Tuesday, after dinner, something changed...

It began with family devotions, which the Taborsky family would do every Tuesday night after supper.

Life had gotten very busy once Johnathon began high school. He would often have to stay late for a sport's practice or game. But, Mr. Taborsky made it very clear that no matter what, every Tuesday, they would have family devotions together.

So, after Mrs. Taborsky's typical taco Tuesday meal, Mr. Taborsky brought out his Bible.

"We will be going through the Ten Commandments this summer," he said.

"Don't we all already *know* the Ten Commandments, Dad?"

Johnathon asked. "I mean, we have them listed in our living room."

This was true. The Taborskys have a framed Ten Commandments hanging in their living room on their chocolate-brown painted wall.

"We may know them, but we need to be reminded of them often. Sometimes we forget what they mean or why God has given them to us," Mr. Taborsky responded. "As we go through them this summer, I pray that we are reminded of God's grace, turn to Jesus, and learn how to love God and others better."

As he spoke, Mr. Taborsky opened his Bible to the book of Exodus, "The first commandment is found in Exodus 20:3. It says,

'You shall have no other gods before me.'"

After his dad read the verse, Timmy thought, *No big deal, that's an easy commandment to follow! I know that there is only one God—I've been told that my whole life!*

But Mr. Taborsky wasn't finished, "With this commandment, it is important we understand God isn't just commanding us to *know* that He is the only god, but He is commanding us to *live* with Him as our only God."

"What do you mean?" Timmy asked.

"God requires Himself to be put first in our hearts and minds, above all else. We need to ask ourselves why we do the things we do. Do we do things because we love ourselves, other people, or a certain thing? Or do we do them because we love God?" Mr. Taborsky asked.

These questions made Timmy start to think.

Mr. Taborsky went on, "Our love for people or things can very easily be put before our love for God, becoming like a god in our lives."

Timmy quickly realized that he had been putting something very obviously before God: baseball.

As the Taborsky family continued to talk, Timmy began to feel very sad. He loved baseball. *Do I have to get rid of baseball in my life?* he thought.

He decided to ask a question out loud, "If I think about baseball more than God sometimes, do I have to stop playing or thinking about it completely?"

Mr. Taborsky looked at Timmy with kind eyes, "Sometimes we do need to totally give up things to fully obey God, but other times we simply need to ask God to help us correct the way we think and feel about things like baseball."

Mrs. Taborsky jumped in, "Loving baseball isn't a bad thing, and working hard to be good at something isn't bad either. But, our lives are all about God, and baseball and all that comes with it needs to be about God too, Timmy."

Timmy listened closely as his parents talked, trying his best to understand. He really didn't want to have any other gods in his life besides the one, true God.

The Taborsky family closed their family devotions with prayer.

As Timmy went to bed later that night, he knew that he was truly committed to baseball, but he wanted to be committed to God above all things, even above baseball.

He wanted God to be the reason he woke up in the morning. He wanted God to be praised for the body he was able to use as he swung his arm to play catch with his brother.

He also wanted to know God more and realized knowing Him better was worth more than knowing the sport of baseball. He knew this might mean sometimes giving up watching a baseball game on TV to read his new Bible he had gotten for his birthday this past year.

These changes did not seem very easy, or that they would happen magically overnight. But that Tuesday, as Timmy laid in bed, he prayed, "God forgive me for putting baseball first in my heart."

Closing his eyes to fall asleep, his prayer continued, "And please help me to love you better and be totally committed to You above all other things!"

Chapter 2

School is finally wrapping up for the year, and every home that has school-aged children is filled with celebration... at least by the kids.

Hopeful dreams of what the next two and a half months would bring filled the minds of each child as they began to make lists of everything they want to do with their time—from building time machines out of cardboard, sticks, and duct tape; to going to the drive-in with visiting cousins.

Each kid had high expectations that this would be the best summer ever! And the Taborsky children were no exception.

It was the end of the school day on Monday, the last day! Timmy and Johnathon excitingly hopped in the car with their mom.

"It's summerrrr!" she said with an excited, sing-songy voice as Johnathon buckled in the front seat and Timmy in the back.

"Woohoo!" Timmy exclaimed while Johnathon reached back to give him a high-five.

On the way home, Mrs. Taborsky drove through the Mr. Munchy's drive-thru for the annual "We made it through another year!" ice cream cone. The creamy treat was the perfect way to celebrate such an occasion.

Just as they were pulling in their driveway, Timmy finished the best part of his cone—the little criss-cross section at the very bottom. Timmy always pushed the vanilla ice cream down with his tongue as he went so that each little square of the cone was full, and the last bite was the perfect combination of creamy and crunchy.

Grabbing his book bag, he entered the house, flung his shoes off on the back porch, and ran to his bedroom.

Once he placed his backpack down on his desk chair, he picked up his Bible and jumped on his bed belly-flop style, landing with his head facing his pillow.

Timmy had been trying to make a habit of going right to his room after school this past week to spend at least five minutes reading his Bible. This was one of the ways he was trying to better obey the first commandment the Taborskys had read about the week before.

Once he realized that he was treating baseball more like a god than God Himself, his parents helped him come up with ideas of how to put God first in his heart and mind. Reading his Bible more was at the top of that list.

Before Timmy opened his Bible, he always liked to pray to ask God to help him understand His Word.

The Bible often seemed confusing, and even when Timmy did understand what he read, it was hard to stay focused. His mind would easily wander to the Spice Lake Salamanders and the first practice that was later that week. Or, his eyes would see a bird out of his window, and he would imagine what it would be like to live a life with wings. Or he would... well, you get the idea, he got easily distracted.

So, Timmy would begin his devotions with prayer. To help him from getting distracted when he prayed, Timmy also closed his eyes.

Another thing that Timmy did while praying was picture what God might look like. It's hard to talk and listen to someone you can't see, so Timmy found it helpful to think of God looking like his dad.

Timmy thought this was a good idea because God is often called our Father. Plus, Timmy's father was a pretty great guy. Sure he wasn't perfect, but he loved Jesus, led the Taborsky family well, and was the strongest person that Timmy could think of—so Timmy figured he was a good person to picture while he was praying.

Once he prayed, he opened his Bible to the book of Psalms. His mom had suggested reading through parts of Psalms because King David's heart of worship is a good example of how we, too, should give attention and praise to God.

After his devotions, Timmy closed his Bible, jumped down from his bed, grabbed his baseball glove, and headed to the yard to play catch. He didn't bother stopping to put his shoes on, because it had finally gotten warm enough to be barefoot outside.

That evening, after they had cleaned up from their scrumptious dinner of perfectly grilled burgers and homemade sweet potato fries, Timmy watched a show with his parents. The show went a little later than his normal bedtime, but he was allowed to finish it because school nights were now a thing of the past... at least for a little while.

———◆———

The first official full day of summer break was one for the books!

After a chocolate chip pancake breakfast, Timmy's mom

took him and Rose Marie to the county's public pool. Timmy's best friend, Bryce, was there as well.

They swam and played Sharks and Minnows for hours, only taking a break to eat their packed lunches.

When they got home, Timmy ran to his room. After changing from his wet clothes, he did his devotions, just like the day before. While he read his Bible, his mom began preparing the typical Taborsky taco Tuesday meal.

Dinner was served and devoured, and then it was time for family devotions.

Timmy's dad once again opened the Bible to Exodus 20, "This week we will be reading the second commandment,

> *'You shall not make for yourself an image in the form of anything in heaven above or on the earth beneath or in the waters below. You shall not bow down to them or worship them; for I, the LORD your God, am a jealous God...'"*

As Timmy listened, he thought, *Who would worship anything that they made?* He remembered from Sunday school talking about the Israelites worshipping the golden calf they had made, but he had never done anything like that.

Timmy's dad continued to explain this commandment. But, he kept getting interrupted by Rose Marie.

First, she was picking her nose. Then she wouldn't stop playing with the tomatoes she left on her plate from dinner. Next, she kept saying, "Hmmmph, how atrocious!" after anyone else spoke (this was a phrase she had picked up from one of the princess shows she loved to watch).

Between all the unplanned pauses, Timmy was still able to learn that the first commandment was mostly about *who* we worshipped and that this commandment was mostly about *how* we worshipped.

Mr. Taborsky said, "We are to only worship God. We are not to worship him by worshipping anything that is made or seen, except Jesus. Actually, Jesus is the only One through whom we can truly worship God."

Timmy had so many questions rolling around in his head!

But before he could ask anything, Johnathon asked one, "I thought Jesus *was* God?"

Timmy's dad agreed, "He is. Jesus is the visible image of the invisible God. God had to send Himself, God the Son, to Earth so that humans could worship Him and have a right relationship with Him."

To this, Rose Marie again responded with her new catchphrase, "Hmmmph, how atrocious!" not even knowing what it meant.

In frustration, Mr. Taborsky slammed his hand down on the table and sharply yelled, "Rose Marie, go to your room! Right now!"

In her dramatic yet understandable fashion, she burst into tears and ran to her bedroom.

Timmy's mom flashed a glance towards his dad that asked, *Was that really necessary?* and ran after Rose Marie, leaving the boys at the table.

After a few moments of sitting in silence, Mr. Taborsky slowly stood up and left the table to go to Rose Marie's room as well.

As Johnathon and Timmy were left at the table, Timmy began to wonder, *Does God lose his patience like my dad? I mean, if He looks like him, He must act like him too...*

A few minutes later, the three came out of Rose Marie's bedroom. They each seemed fine, though everyone was much quieter the rest of the evening.

That night, as Timmy was climbing into bed, his dad entered the room. Once Timmy was under his covers, his dad sat down on the edge of his comforter, "Timmy, I need to ask for your forgiveness. I acted wrongly in my anger tonight towards your sister, and you were a part of that. Please forgive me for not responding correctly."

Timmy responded with a quick but rather quiet, "Of course, Dad, I forgive you!"

"Thank you, Son," his dad said in return. He bent down to kiss Timmy on the forehead, "Goodnight."

But before he stood up all the way, Timmy asked, "Hey Dad, do you think God looks like you?"

With a surprised look on his face, his dad asked, "What do you mean?"

Timmy explained, "Well, when I pray, I find it helpful to picture what God looks like. And because we sometimes call God our Father, and you're my father, I picture you when I talk to Him."

Timmy's dad sat back down and thought for a minute, "Actually Timmy, God the Father doesn't have a form. He is Spirit. Remember the commandment that I read earlier?"

"Yes," Timmy said.

"Well, putting a picture, *any* picture, to God other than Jesus, God the Son, is breaking that commandment," Mr. Taborsky responded.

"Really?" Timmy asked with worry.

"Yes. I struggle with obeying this commandment sometimes

too, but when we disobey in this way, we are putting God in a box. We are comparing Him to something way less and imperfect. God is the perfect Father, Timmy, and I am very far from perfect. You saw that earlier tonight in the way I responded to your sister at the dinner table."

Timmy didn't really know what to think about this, "So how am I supposed to pray to God without having a picture in my mind?"

Mr. Taborsky responded through a soft, thoughtful smile, "Like with everything, we should ask God to help us. We also need to remember we have been given a great gift in the Bible. God tells us everything we need to know about Himself inside the pages of His Word. What we read, should shape our thoughts about Him."

"Okay..." Timmy said with a big sigh.

"Let's ask Him for help right now together," Mr. Taborksy said as he closed his eyes and grabbed Timmy's hand. "God, we need Your help. May we not picture You in any way that isn't right. Help us know who You are better so that we can worship You without our sinful, human thoughts of who You might be getting in the way. Please help us decide to read Your Word more so we can know You better. In Jesus' name, amen."

"Thanks, Dad," Timmy said. "I love you!"

"Love you too, Timmy," Mr. Taborksy said, turning off the lights and closing the door behind him.

Lying there in bed, Timmy did feel better. He was still unsure about how he would pray moving forward, but one thing he was sure about was that God would help him.

With that thought, Timmy closed his eyes and fell asleep.

Chapter 3

S ummer is now in full swing, which means the bottoms of feet have gotten used to walking on hot driveways and pebbled grass, and eating popsicles in the heat of the afternoon is more of a pattern than a surprise treat.

This also means that Timmy has already had two baseball practices with the Spice Lake Salamanders, and he has absolutely loved them!

His coach, Coach Mark, is super kind and super encouraging. Timmy actually knows him from church because he teaches Large Group in Sunday school once a month.

Bryce, Timmy's best friend, is also on his team, which makes everything even more exciting!

And, if that isn't enough, Timmy was asked to be one of the main pitchers—the very position that he wanted!

All the months of waiting and anticipation were well worth it. Timmy could tell that this was going to be the perfect baseball season... well, almost perfect.

There is one thing, or one person really, that is stopping Timmy's Spice Lake Salamander experience from perfection: Glenn.

Glenn goes to the same school as Timmy, and is in the same grade, though he had a different teacher. But, Timmy knew enough about Glenn to know he didn't really want him on his baseball team.

Glenn is a quieter kid and doesn't talk to others a whole lot. He never seems to have clean hair or clean clothes. Timmy was actually really surprised that he even signed up for base-ball because, during recess at school, he would always be by himself under a tree drawing with a stick in the dirt.

After the first two practices, it became clear that Glenn may have never even touched a baseball. When he threw the ball, it's almost as though he had no grip. The ball would go in every direction but where it needed to be. And when he tried to catch the ball, he would just stick his glove up and close his eyes, that is if he didn't trip before he made it to where he thought the ball might land.

Glenn was going to hold the Spice Lake Salamanders back, and everyone knew it.

On Tuesday, Mr. Taborsky pulled up to the Spice Lake com-munity baseball fields as the Spice Lake Salamanders' practice was wrapping up. Timmy and Bryce piled in the car after the team huddle, where Coach Mark had given them the three things they did well and what they needed to work on for their next practice.

The boys opened the door and piled in the backseat. "How was practice, boys?" Mr. Taborsky asked.

Timmy let out a big sigh, and once his seatbelt was clicked into place, he said, "Great, except *someone* can't seem to catch a single ball!"

Bryce piped in too, "Oh my! It was *so* bad! It's like he has butterfingers or something!"

Timmy and Bryce went on for a minute or so. It started

with complaining about Glenn's lack of talent and then became just mean comments about Glenn.

Mr. Taborsky finally said, "Alright, boys, that's enough." He then asked, "Hey Bryce, how would you like to join us for dinner? I can call your parents and see if we could just drop you off afterward."

Timmy piped up, "Yes! Oh please! Can you ask if he can spend the night too?!"

Mr. Taborsky chuckled at Timmy's excitement, "He can't spend the night tonight, but I'll see if this Friday or next would work for a sleepover when I call."

Timmy and Bryce looked at each other and pumped their arms back and forth as they both whispered, "Yes! Yes! Yes!" over and over again.

Bryce's parents agreed that he could stay for dinner.

Because Bryce was a pickier eater than Timmy or his siblings, Mrs. Taborsky set aside a special plate of non-seasoned meat just for Bryce as she prepared the typical Taborsky taco Tuesday meal.

As dinner wrapped up, it was again time for family devotions.

"Bryce, we're going through the Ten Commandments this summer as a family," Mrs. Taborsky explained.

This wasn't weird for Bryce because he came from a family that loved Jesus and attended the same church as the Taborskys.

"Honey, would you want to read the commandment this week?" Mr. Taborsky asked Mrs. Taborsky.

"I'd love to," she responded.

Being a school librarian, Mrs. Taborsky is used to reading aloud, and she always did so with a sweet, clear voice, "Here we are, Exodus 20:7,

*'You shall not misuse the name of the LORD your
God, for the LORD will not hold anyone guiltless
who misuses his name.'"*

After Mrs. Taborsky finished reading, Rose Marie burst out
with a question, "What does 'misuse' mean?!"

Mr. Taborsky responded, with much more patience than
the week before, "Well, if you hear, the word *'use'* is in there,
but *'mis'* is before it. So, *'misuse'* means to wrongly use something. This commandment is saying we aren't to use God's
name in a wrong way."

Timmy was pretty smug with himself. He thought, *Finally,
a commandment I've actually been obeying!* Timmy had been
trained to never use God's name as a curse word or a form of
selfish excitement his whole life.

He even felt confident enough to speak up, "Well, I think
we all follow that commandment really well!"

Johnathon agreed with a quick, "Yeah, me too!"

Their dad tilted his head towards Timmy, "Hmmm, do you?"

Timmy responded, this time with a little less confidence
because of the way his dad asked the question, "Well yeah,
I mean, you've always taught us not to say God's name in a
wrong way."

"I'm so glad that's true, but there is more to this command
than just not using God's name incorrectly."

"Like what?" Johnathon asked.

Mr. Taborsky went on to explain, "If we claim to be God's
children, we are called to a high standard. When we repent of
our sins and turn to Jesus as our Savior and Lord, we not only
bear God's image as His creation but also carry His name as

His children. And, as His children, we are to do our best to reflect His character."

"Okay..." Timmy said, not fully understanding.

"Yes, we have to be careful not to use God's name wrongly,
but we also can't claim to be God's children and then live how-
ever we want. We are commanded to *act* like we know and
follow God when we say with our mouths that we *do* know
and follow Him," said Mr. Taborsky.

Timmy still felt as though he followed this commandment
pretty well. *People know I'm a Christian, and I act like one
too. I listen to all my teachers, and I never cheat in school,* he
thought.

The Taborskys and Bryce prayed, and then cleaned up the
table.

Once the table was clear, it was time to take Bryce back
home, and Timmy went with.

Pulling out of the driveway, Mr. Taborsky asked, "So boys,
are there any ways that you feel you have been struggling to
keep the commandment that we talked about tonight?"

Before Timmy could say anything, Bryce said in a guilty
tone, "Yes."

Timmy was shocked!

Bryce continued, "As you explained what the commandment meant, I couldn't help but think that we did not show that
we follow God with the way we talked about Glenn earlier
today."

Timmy, all of a sudden, felt like a rock hit the bottom of his
stomach. He hadn't even thought of that!

Mr. Taborsky replied in a gentle voice, "Wow Bryce, I'm really glad God showed you that. I do believe you're right. Boys,

what you said earlier, was very unkind. You both sounded like bullies."

Timmy and Bryce looked down at their feet as Mr. Taborsky continued, "God created Glenn, and your words did not show God's love for Glenn at all. I know both of you have made a decision to follow Jesus, and because of that, you have to be careful with your words. People should know God more after interacting with you, not want less to do with Him because of the way you behave."

Mr. Taborsky saw Timmy and Bryce's eyes start to fill with tears, "We all have ways in which we need to work on obeying God and keeping His name holy. I, too, fail to show God to others with the way I act all the time. I have been thinking about how I need to be careful with my attitude at work."

"How about we pray together?" Mr. Taborky asked.

"Yes," Timmy and Bryce responded together.

For the rest of the drive, Mr. Taborsky led a prayer, "God, thank You for Your grace and patience with us as Your children. Please forgive us for the ways we misuse and misrepresent Your name. Please help us obey Your Spirit so we can follow you in *every* way with our *whole* lives. We cannot do this on our own and need Your help! In Jesus' name, amen."

Timmy and Bryce agreed with every word that was prayed, and Timmy could already feel his frustration with Glenn melting away.

Hmmm, maybe this summer with the Spice Lake Salamanders will be the best ever, he thought as he waved goodbye to Bryce.

Chapter 4

It's now July in the town of Spice Lake, and the temperature and humidity seem to rise with each day. This weather makes for great days at the pool and great evenings fishing on the shore of Spice Lake.

July also brought the first game for Timmy's baseball team. It was quite the experience. The game was against the Tortoise Lake Tornados, and the Salamanders won by two runs!

Timmy absolutely loves most parts of summer, but he is beginning to feel exhausted.

This kind of tired isn't from the extreme heat and the countless hours of practicing baseball. Nor is it from his big imagination that took him to space as an astronaut with his best friend Bryce in their homemade rocket ship. It isn't even from going to bed a little later each night because he didn't have school the next morning.

No, this form of tired Timmy felt in his heart and mind.

With the Taborksys going through the Ten Commandments, Timmy has realized that he doesn't keep them very well at all. He has tried really hard to make changes to his life. He has started reading his Bible every day. He is trying to remember God the Father is different than his dad. And he is doing his best to be kind with his words, especially about Glenn, so that he can show God's heart to others.

But trying to do all these things wipes Timmy out. He feels like he is constantly trying his hardest but still constantly failing and letting God down.

Timmy was sure God was disappointed with him. How could he not be?

It's because of these feelings, Timmy has started to lose a lot of his excitement about summer. He thought it would be better to stay in his room so that he didn't see as many people and didn't have as many chances to break the commandments God has given.

Mrs. Taborsky could tell Timmy's attitude changed. He was talking less at breakfast and stopped asking to hang out with Bryce every afternoon.

After about two days of noticing things weren't normal for Timmy, Mrs. Taborsky went to Timmy's room after breakfast.

"Timmy, are you doing okay?" she asked as she softly opened Timmy's bedroom door and stood right inside. "You don't seem to be acting like yourself the past couple days."

Timmy, who was reading on his bed, shrugged his shoulders and said, "Yeah, I'm fine."

The way he said it clearly showed his mom that he was *not* doing fine.

Mrs. Taborsky sat down on his bed and patted his back, "Why don't you put the book down for a minute, Timmy."

Timmy turned toward his mom, and she continued to talk, "I don't think you're really doing fine, Sweetie. You have been spending a lot more time by yourself in your room. Are you sad about something?"

Timmy sat up all the way and let out a big sigh, "Well," he began as he looked towards the ground, "I just can't seem to obey God and follow all his commands very well, Mom."

"What do you mean, Timmy?" she asked.

"I've been trying super hard to change and follow the commandments that we've talked about, but I just keep messing up! I mean, there are times I do really well, but I haven't gone a whole day without saying something mean or thinking about baseball more than God."

He took another big sigh, and with the exhale, rested his hands in between his fists, "I'm just *sure* I'm letting God down..."

"You're right," Mrs. Taborsky said very matter-of-factly, but still with her soft, loving tone.

Timmy looked up at his mom with an extremely worried look, "I am?".

She placed her hand on Timmy's back, "Well, kind of, Sweetie. Every one of us is unable to follow God's commands perfectly. God has a perfect standard, and all of us are unable to meet that standard: you, me, your dad, all of us."

"Then what's the point of even trying?" asked Timmy.

"That's a great question. God knew that we were not going to be able to keep His commands perfectly. Since Adam and Eve, we have all had a sinful nature, which makes it impossible for us to meet God's expectations of perfection. That's why He sent Jesus. He is the *only* person who has ever perfectly obeyed all of God's commands. And his death was the price that He willingly paid for all those who believe in Him as Lord and Savior."

"So, I don't have to keep all the commands?" Timmy asked a little confused.

"We are still commanded to follow God and obey the rules He has given us. But we don't obey to *earn* His love, we obey to *show* our love for Him. The commandments help us realize our need for Jesus. When we realize our need, we turn away from our sin to Him in what we call repentance. We're then given the gift of the Holy Spirit, who helps us better know and obey God. Does that make sense?"

"I think so," Timmy said.

"And the really cool thing is we can find great joy in knowing Jesus kept all the commandments perfectly. He fully met all of God's expectations. When we believe Jesus is the only One who can save us from our sins and allow Him to be King of our lives, he covers us. This means God sees us as He sees Jesus: holy and without sin!"

Timmy's face changed from worry to amazement, "Wow! That is really cool!"

"It really is," Mrs. Taborsky smiled at her son's change in attitude. "Now, why don't you come help me make a strawberry pie for later today?"

Timmy happily followed his mom to the kitchen. He felt so much better. The heavy weight that he felt on his heart seemed to have been picked up and thrown off!

Rose Marie joined Timmy and Mrs. Taborsky in the kitchen. By the end of the pie-making process, there was flour covering each of them.

Once they cleaned up their mess, Timmy enjoyed the rest of the day. He was back to his normal, summer-loving self.

That evening, after the typical taco Tuesday meal, Mr. Taborsky pulled out the Bible for family devotions.

Timmy got a little nervous, *What commandment am I going to have to think through now?* he wondered.

Mr. Taborsky opened His Bible, "Tonight we are reading from Exodus 20 again, starting in verse eight:

> *'Remember the Sabbath day by keeping it holy. Six days you shall labor and do all your work, but the seventh day is a sabbath to the LORD your God. On it you shall not do any work... For in six days the LORD made the heavens and the earth, the sea, and all that is in them, but he rested on the seventh day. Therefore the LORD blessed the Sabbath day and made it holy.'"*

Timmy was confused with all that meant, but Mrs. Taborsky spoke up right away, "Timmy, this commandment reminds me of the conversation we had earlier today!"

"It does?" Timmy asked.

"Yes! Oh, I was just listening to a sermon the other day that did a great job explaining how the Sabbath really points us to Jesus! Rest is a very important part of life—we obviously need it to take care of our bodies. But, even more importantly, we need to rest in Jesus—in who He is and what He has done. Like I was telling you earlier, Timmy, we can't work hard enough to earn God's approval, but instead, we need to fully trust in Jesus."

Listening to his mom explain this commandment brought so much joy and peace to Timmy.

"What a wonderful truth!" Mr. Taborsky declared. "God is so loving and kind to provide what we need in Jesus."

"You can say that again!" Timmy exclaimed.

"Ummmm, is it time for pie yet?" Rose Marie chimed in.

"Yes, I believe it is," Mrs. Taborsky said as she stood up to grab the pie from the refrigerator.

The pie was delicious, and Timmy couldn't think of another pie that ever tasted as sweet. Maybe it was because Rose Marie had been in charge of counting the cups of sugar, or maybe it was because Timmy was so full of joy knowing he could rest in Jesus. Either way, he ate every last crumb that was on his plate.

When bedtime arrived, Timmy snuggled under his covers and let out a prayer of praise, "God, thank You so much that because of Jesus, You aren't disappointed with me. Thank you that Jesus has made things right, and I can rest in Him!"

That night, Timmy really did rest well, both physically *and* spiritually.

Chapter 5

S ummer is going faster than anyone could imagine and it's nearly halfway through.

Timmy already has a tan line from wearing his blue watch he had gotten to go with his Spice Lake Salamander uniform.

Speaking of the Spice Lake Salamanders, they have been doing pretty well. They have won four out of the five games they have played.

During their last game, Glenn caught a ball, giving their opponents the last out to end the game. He had gotten a lot better over the past two months and has even joined Bryce and Timmy once on a Friday afternoon when they practiced in Bryce's yard.

Yes, summer is a season that brings many new, fun things like baseball for Timmy. But, one thing that doesn't change from season to season in the Taborsky household is Saturday chores.

Saturday chores have been in place as long as Timmy could remember. Every Saturday, after an allowed half-hour of cartoons, each Taborsky child is responsible to clean. Each week the tasks remained the same.

Johnathon, after cleaning his own room, is in charge of dusting and vacuuming the living room.

Timmy, after cleaning his own room, is in charge of wiping down the dining room table and then sweeping and mopping the floor.

Rose Marie, only being four, and having had an incident with some of Mrs. Taborsky's favorite set of dishes a few weeks ago, is simply in charge of cleaning her own room.

These chores were required to get done every Saturday, every week, in every season... even summer. This Saturday is no different.

As soon as Samuel and his brothers from the show *Samuel and the Squirrels* finished singing the closing song in their usual three-part harmony, Timmy turned off the TV.

Everyone already knew that it was time to begin chores, but just in case anyone forgot, Mr. Taborsky walked in the living room and enthusiastically said, "Let's go, let's go, let's go! Teamwork makes the dream work!" clapping his hands continuously as though he was a coach prepping his team for the final quarter.

Johnathon and Timmy both quickly got up and rushed to their rooms. They had learned that if they worked hard and didn't lollygag, they could finish their chores in less than an hour. This gave them more time to do other things later in the day.

Rose Marie, on the other hand, had yet to learn these things, and on this particular Saturday, she seemed to be dragging her feet even *more* than usual.

"Come on, Rose Marie! You have some stuffed animals that need to go back to their play pin, I think!" said Mr. Taborsky, trying to motivate the little girl that was still sitting on the couch, twirling her hair between her fingers.

Rose Marie slowly slid off the couch to her feet. With a great big sigh, she said, "Okay, daddy, I'm goooooiiiiing." She trotted down the hall to her room, which was right across the hallway from Timmy's bedroom.

Once she finally made it through her doorway, Timmy could see that she was not quickly going to work on putting her stuffed animals away. Instead, he saw her make a scrunched up face while lying on her bed, saying to herself, "I'm ne-ver going to make *my* children clean their rooms!".

Rose Marie pouted for quite some time, until Mrs. Taborsky said, "Let's keep moving little Missy!" as she zipped passed her room on her way to take a fifth load of laundry down to the washer.

Rose Marie slowly, and sassily, began to pick up her stuffed animals, one at a time.

By the time Rose Marie picked up her fourth stuffed animal to drag it across the room to her toy chest, Timmy had already finished cleaning his room and moved to the dining room.

By eleven o'clock, Johnathon and Timmy were both done with their chores and were outside enjoying the sun. But not Rose Marie.

If you were to peak in Rose Marie's room, you wouldn't have noticed anything different than earlier that day. In fact, while putting her stuffed mermaid in the toy chest, she spotted her tea set and began a tea party on the floor with the remaining stuffed animals that were spread around her room.

By lunchtime, Rose Marie was still not done. The longer she made the process, the more she didn't want to do it, and the more she believed it was an impossible task.

After many redirections, corrections, and a timer finally being set, Rose Marie finished around three o'clock that afternoon. Sadly, she had spent most of her Saturday avoiding cleaning her room by pouting and dragging her feet with each little task. She even missed out on going to the park with her friend Michelle earlier because she wasn't finished with her room.

———◆———

The rest of the weekend came and went, and the week started off with nothing too out of the ordinary.

It was now Tuesday night, and the Taborskys were finishing up their typical taco Tuesday meal.

Mr. Taborsky pulled out his Bible and turned to where he had it marked, "Exodus 20:12 is where the fifth commandment is found. It says,

> *'Honor your father and your mother, so that you may live long in the land the LORD your God is giving you.'*

"Well, we alllll better remember this one!" Mr. Taborsky said in a joking tone as he winked at Mrs. Taborsky.

He went on, "But truly, honoring your parents is something that God commands each of His children to do."

"What are some ways that you think you can honor your dad and me?" Mrs. Taborsky asked.

"By obeying you both," Timmy responded.

"And by being kind and thankful," Johnathon chimed in.

"Yes! Those are both great ways, boys," Mr. Taborsky replied.

Mrs. Taborsky then added, "An important truth about obedience I learned when I was young, was that obedience that pleases the Lord isn't *just* finishing a certain task. True obedience involves our hearts."

"That's right," Mr. Taborsky said. "God desires true obedience, and that includes making sure our attitudes are in the right place, *along* with our actions."

The Taborskys ended their time with prayer, as usual, cleaned up the table, and relaxed the rest of the evening.

While brushing his teeth before bed, Timmy was reminded of what had happened that past Saturday. He remembered how Rose Marie finally cleaned her room, but she didn't do it right away or with a good attitude. He also remembered that she didn't get to play with her friend as a consequence of not obeying right away.

This made Timmy think through ways in which his heart wasn't always right in obeying his mom or dad.

Before falling asleep that night, Timmy talked to God, "Dear Lord, please help me not just *do* the right thing, but do the right thing *with* the right attitude as I try to honor and obey my mom and dad. In Jesus' name, amen."

"Oh, wait!" he continued, "I should ask the same thing about obeying You! Please help me to obey You always, right away, and with the right heart. I want to honor You too. Okay, I think that's all for today."

And with that honest prayer, Timmy turned to his side and dozed off to sleep.

Chapter 6

In Timmy's seven-year-old world, very few things seem more exciting than going to see a movie on the big screen. There is something about watching a movie you have never seen before come to life right before your eyes in a cold building with the smell of popcorn in the air.

This was an experience that didn't happen very often for Timmy, which made it all the more exciting when it did happen. And, on this particular Tuesday in July, the Taborskys planned a trip to their local theater.

Because they were going to the movies, their normal Tuesday evening plans were changed.

Instead of Mrs. Taborsky making their typical taco Tuesday meal, she cut up some venison sausage and cheese for everyone to munch on earlier than their normal dinner time. She insisted everyone eat some because popcorn would not be a sufficient dinner.

As soon as Mr. Taborsky got home from work, showered off, and changed, the Taborskys were off to the Spice Lake 5 Theater.

They arrived about a half-hour before the movie began, and it was a good thing they did. In Spice Lake on Tuesdays, the theater shows movies at a discount. This is why a lot of families choose to go on Tuesdays, and today was no exception.

When they arrived, Mrs. Taborsky waited in line for tickets while Mr. Taborsky headed straight for the popcorn line. All of the Taborskys loved popcorn, but no one loved it as much as Mr. Taborsky. He always said, "Popcorn with a movie, is like a dance that's extra groovy!"

Timmy didn't really know what "groovy" meant, but he was okay with it because he did know the phrase meant he could always count on having popcorn with a movie if his dad was around.

Once the tickets were bought, and the popcorn buckets were filled, with extra butter and salt, of course, the Taborskys rushed to find a row of five seats all together.

Between Rose Marie choosing who she wanted to sit by, the passing out of napkins, and the distribution of the popcorn, it took about five minutes for everyone to get settled in their seats. They were all comfortable right in time for the official previews to start.

Then the real movie began. Timmy looked down the row at his family with a big smile and then back up at the screen with excitement as the title flashed on the black screen: *THE KOALA KING.*

The movie tells the story of a young koala named Kingston. He was born to a very poor, but very kind family that lived within the Fern Forest Kingdom. Kingston's parents both worked in a factory that made shields for the knights that protected their King.

When Kingston was just a young joey, he went with his parents to work. As they worked, his mom and dad would tell stories where they pretended Kingston was the King of the Fern Forest Kingdom. They would tell of heroic battles he won, of daring deeds he performed, and the kindness he spread to both the rich and the poor.

When Kingston grew older, he trained hard and actually became one of the knights that used the very shields he once helped his parents make.

During this time, a small group of evil wallabies decided to revolt against the King. This group was led by the most wicked wallaby of all: Wallace.

Wallace had a story of his own. He, too, grew up in a poor family, but his parents were not kind and humble at heart like Kingston's. From a young age, Wallace grew in hatred for the King because he did not understand how someone could be so wealthy while others, like his family, went hungry.

This heart of hatred grew in Wallace, and he desired to one day take the throne away from the King and become the king himself.

Wallace eventually did take the throne away from the King by killing him. But, Kingston fought bravely against Wallace to protect the people in the Fern Forest Kingdom. Kingston led the knights into battle, eventually capturing Wallace and punishing him by placing him in the castle's dungeon.

Kingston was rewarded greatly for his bravery, and the tales he grew up listening to became a reality as Kingston became the Koala King!

As the Taborskys watched, they took turns gasping, laughing, jumping, and of course, there were a couple times Rose Marie whimpered. But, Timmy didn't blame her, because there were a few scary parts.

Once the movie was over, the Taborskys stood up into the "after movie stretch" everyone seems to do at the theater—leading up with both arms and ending with a big yawn.

After gathering all their items, which took another five minutes, they stopped by the bathroom and then loaded back up into the car.

"What did you guys think?" Mr. Taborsky asked when they were all buckled in.

"It was great! Thanks for taking us, Dad," Timmy replied.

Johnathon agreed, and so did Rose Marie, but she added, "But Wallace was scary!"

"He sure was!" Mrs. Taborsky agreed.

"You know," Mr. Taborsky started thoughtfully, "Wallace's behavior is a good example of what it looks like when we break the sixth commandment. Estelle, would you look up Exodus 20:13?"

"I'd be glad to," Mrs. Taborsky took her phone and scrolled to Exodus 20:13. She read,

"'You shall not murder.'"

"That's the shortest commandment yet, I think," said Johnathon. "That's a verse I definitely think I can memorize."

"Yes, it's pretty short," Mr. Taborsky said, "*and* a very important commandment to follow."

"Well, Wallace did not follow that commandment, did he?" Rose Marie said as she crossed her arms and shook her head back and forth.

"He sure didn't," Mrs. Taborsky agreed as she looked at Rose Marie's reflection through the rearview mirror.

"You would have to be pretty awful to actually murder someone in real life, right?" Timmy asked.

"Right," Mr. Taborsky replied. "But Jesus actually transforms this commandment in the New Testament. He tells us in one of His sermons that God not only commands us not to kill unjustly, but He commands us to not have anger in our hearts towards others, specifically other members of God's family."

"Wallace is a good warning of what disobeying this commandment leads to," Mr. Taborsky continued. "He was hurt by others and didn't deal with his pain in the right way. This led to anger and hate, and ended up leading to murder."

Mrs. Taborsky added with her sweet voice, "We need to always be asking God to check our hearts and emotions towards others. If we don't allow God to change our wrong feelings, it very well could lead to hate, which Jesus says is as bad as murder."

"Wow, that's a big deal!" Timmy said as he was trying to think through all that was said.

Everyone agreed.

"Do you think the story would have ended differently if Wallace would have forgiven the King for not helping the poor?" Mr. Taborsky asked.

"Most definitely," Johnathon said, "The whole ending would have been different."

"Living in sin may feel good in the moment, but it is never worth it," Mr. Taborsky said in conclusion to Wallace's actions. "He definitely paid for the wicked things that he did."

"Ummm, did we just do family devotions in the car?" Rose Marie asked with a scrunched up face.

Everyone giggled a little at Rose Marie's discovery while Timmy looked over at her and said, "I think so!"

"Will you end our evening with prayer, Johnathon?" Mr. Taborsky asked, "Asking God to fill our hearts with love for others and helping us be quick to forgive as God has forgiven us."

"Sure," Johnathon began, "Dear God, thank you for letting us go to the movies tonight. Thank you for the Bible. Please help us to follow you by not killing others, even with the way we feel towards them in our heart or with our thoughts. May we be quick to ask for help from You when we feel anger in our hearts. In Jesus' name, amen."

The whole Taborsky clan agreed as they pulled into the driveway with an "Amen."

Chapter 7

July has passed, and August has begun, bringing more rain and storms than usual to Spice Lake and the surrounding towns.

The rain has caused the Taborskys to be indoors more than they have been all summer, and Mrs. Taborsky found this to be the perfect opportunity to encourage her children to read.

Johnathon reads pretty thick chapter books—books with no pictures at all. His favorites are historical fiction books that detail wars from American history.

Timmy, though he became a pretty good reader this past year in Mrs. Gorbill's class, still likes the smaller, sillier books—the ones with lots of pictures.

On this Tuesday evening, it was raining outside, and the smell of tacos started to fill the Taborsky's house. Johnathon sat in the oversized chair in the corner reading a book on the Civil War, while Timmy and Rose Marie sat close together on the couch. Timmy read aloud one of his favorites: *Mrs. McLegs Guards Her Eggs*.

The story is about a deep-sea octopus named Mrs. McLegs, who is on a mission to protect her eggs. Once she finds a place to lay her eggs, she puts herself on top of them to shield them from danger and provide oxygen for them to grow.

She stays there over four years—never moving from her spot or getting distracted from her mission. Through the four years, she experiences every season, many visits from scary deep-sea creatures, and strong hunger pains because food isn't always nearby, but not once does she leave her eggs.

As Timmy reads, he and Rose Marie giggle their way through the book. It wasn't so much that the story was funny, but because each page rhymed, it sounded silly.

By the time the story was finished, and Mrs. McLegs' eggs finally hatched, Mr. Taborsky was home. Timmy put the book down and rushed to set the table; it was his turn to do so according to the chore chart that hung on the fridge.

The Taborskys enjoyed their typical taco Tuesday meal together. Mr. and Mrs. Taborsky talked back and forth about the upcoming weather forecast and when might be a good time to mow the lawn and weed the garden.

Conversation then moved to involve everyone. They talked about what they needed for the start of the school year, which they could hardly believe was just around the corner.

Once the meal was over, Mr. Taborsky sent Rose Marie to grab his Bible off his nightstand by his bed.

"Thank you very much!" Mr. Taborsky said once she returned. "Tonight, we will read from Exodus 20:14, the seventh commandment." Finding the verse he read,

"'You shall not commit adultery.'"

"Adultery?" Rose Marie said in her high pitched voice. "Does that mean becoming like an adult?"

Mr. and Mrs. Taborsky shared a smile with each other at Rose Marie's question.

"No, though the word 'adult' is in 'adultery,' so I can see why you would think that, Sweetie," Mrs. Taborsky replied.

"Well, what does it mean then?" Rose Marie asked.

"To commit adultery means to break the promise of staying faithful to the person that you marry," Mr. Taborsky replied.

This time Timmy asked a question, "What do you mean 'staying faithful'?"

Mrs. Taborsky's face lit up at this question, "Remember the story you read to Rose Marie right before dinner?" she asked. "In that story, Mrs. McLegs was faithful. No matter what came, she stayed on her eggs until they hatched. She went through hot, hot summers; and cold, cold winters. There were a lot of things that tempted her to leave her eggs, like hunger or mean fish. But, no matter what, she was disciplined and stayed focused. She was committed to keeping her eggs safe and healthy. That is an example of being faithful."

"Ohhhh, okay," Timmy said, shaking his head.

"Yes, that's a great example," Mr. Taborsky added. "We are to be faithful to the promises made in marriage. And, just like there were hard things Mrs. McLegs went through, there are hard things in marriage too, but God commands us to stay faithful and keep our promises."

"So, is this only for when I grow up and marry a prince?" Rose Marie asked, batting her eyes and flipping her hair.

"Another great question, Rose Marie," Mr. Taborsky said.

Timmy and Johnathon rolled their eyes at their dramatic little sister.

Mr. Taborsky flipped in his Bible, "Let's take a look at another passage. This is Matthew 5:27-28. It says:

> *'You have heard that it was said, 'You shall not commit adultery.' But I tell you that anyone who looks at a woman lustfully has already committed adultery with her in his heart.'*

"This verse has some more big words," Mr. Taborsky acknowledged, "But they are important. Jesus Himself said these words. Did anyone pick up the last word that I read?"

Rose Marie quickly responded, "Heart! That is my favorite shape!" she exclaimed.

"Yes!" Mr. Taborsky replied.

"Great Listening," Mrs. Taborsky winked at Rose Marie, who smiled big at herself for getting the right answer.

Mr. Taborsky continued, "This commandment, like the others, has to do with the heart. It involves our thoughts and emotions. God not *only* commands us to be faithful with our actions in marriage, but He also commands his children to remain faithful with our thoughts, eyes, and time as well, both in marriage *and* outside of marriage."

"God calls His people to be holy, or set-apart from this world, in every way!" Mrs. Taborsky added. "And like your dad said, it isn't always easy. In fact, it's very hard at times. That's why we need each other and why we put boundaries in place."

"Boundaries?" Timmy asked, "Like what do you mean?"

"'Limits' is another word for we use for boundaries," Mrs. Taborsky said.

"Yes, we have TV and screen time limits in our home for

both *what* we watch and *how much* we watch. This is all part of protecting our eyes, thoughts, and emotions," Mr. Taborsky added.

The kids all slowly nodded their heads as their dad finished. They didn't really like TV and screen time limits, but at least they knew it was for a reason.

Mr. Taborsky closed in prayer, and after the table was cleared and wiped down by Johnathon, they finished the night together playing a round of *Number Catch*, their favorite family card game.

After the game, which Johnathon won, it was time for Rose Marie and Timmy to go to bed.

Once Timmy was tucked in, and the lights were out, he reviewed the story of *Mrs. McLegs Guards Her Eggs* again in his head and smiled at the memory of the funny rhyming words.

Though the book was silly to Timmy, he did admire Mrs. McLegs' dedication.

Closing his eyes, Timmy prayed, "God, help me to be like Mrs. McLegs. I mean, of course I don't have any eggs like her, but I want to be faithful like she was faithful. Please help me to be faithful to my wife one day, if I ever do get married...which I'm not so sure about. But even if I don't get married, help me to be faithful to You. Help me to follow You in every way no matter what I go through or how I am tempted. Thanks, God, amen."

And with that prayer, Timmy fell fast asleep.

Chapter 8

After an extremely hot July, August has brought such pleasant afternoons to Spice Lake— ones with a cool breeze that doesn't make it feel like the air is sticking to your sweaty face. It was still warm, but it's what the Taborkys always called "good camping weather" because the idea of a fire at night was actually pleasant, since there was a slight chill in the air when the sun went down.

Timmy was thankful for this change in the weather. He thought it was the perfect weather to play baseball. And, on this Tuesday afternoon, the Spice Lake Salamanders actually had a game!

Timmy's mom dropped him off at the field ten minutes early like usual, because he liked to get a couple of practice swings in before the rest of the team arrived.

He felt good about today, and he felt good about the Spice Lake Salamanders' chance at getting another win.

When he got to the field, he sat down on his team's bench and put his bag down between his feet. Bending down, he unzipped his bag to look for his gum.

Mrs. Taborsky had bought him a mega-pack of gum for his baseball season at the beginning of the summer. He told her it made him feel like a professional baseball player when he chewed it out on the field. He also claimed it helped him stay more focused during the game. So, each practice and each game, Timmy would pop a piece of Watermelon Bubble Gum in his mouth before setting foot on the field.

Timmy unzipped the side pocket of his bag, where he stored his pack of gum—nothing!

Frantically, he unzipped the main part of his bag, sometimes he would accidentally place his gum in there. Searching around with his eyes and hands, he couldn't see or feel a single piece of gum!

Starting to become more frustrated, he realized he must have finished the pack of gum that was in there and forgotten to grab a new one from the stash in his bedroom.

What to do, what to do? Timmy thought to himself.

Timmy decided he would have to ask his mom for a piece when she returned to watch the game. He was disappointed that he didn't have it for his warm-up, but he would have to make do.

After a few minutes, the rest of the team members started showing up and piling their bags on the Spice Lake Salamander's bench before heading to the field to practice.

After a while of throwing the ball to each other, Coach Mark called the team together.

The game was about to start, the seats were filling up, and Timmy was frantically looking around. He didn't see any sign of his mom!

I really need some gum to make sure I do my best for this game, he thought.

While Timmy continued to scan the bleachers, he spotted an open backpack on his team's bench. A bright pink package was resting right on top.

Could it be? he wondered.

Walking towards the bag, it became clear his guess was correct. There, right before his eyes, was a pack of Watermelon Bubble Gum!

By now, the team already had their pregame huddle and were being sent out to the field.

Timmy argued with himself in his head, *I can't take someone else's gum without asking... but I'm sure they wouldn't mind. I mean, I don't really have time to ask. Plus, I'm sure they would want me to have it because it will help us win the game, so it's fine.*

With that thought, Timmy took a piece of gum and headed out to the field.

As soon as he popped that piece of gum in his mouth, it was filled with a burst of juicy watermelon, but with a burst of flavor in his mouth also came an uneasy feeling in his stomach.

Timmy tried to shake the feeling the entire game, but he couldn't.

The Spice Lake Salamanders won, yet Timmy didn't feel like celebrating.

He gathered his stuff and walked to the minivan without talking to any of his teammates. He opened the door and sat in his usual seat without a sound.

"Way to go, Sweetie!" Mrs. Taborsky said with a smile as Timmy closed the door to the back seat.

Rose Marie went into the chant she had made with her mom and screamed every time Timmy had gone to the mound to pitch, "Look at that pitcher, I'm his little sister! Woohoo!"

"Thanks, guys..." Timmy responded with way less enthusiasm than Rose Marie.

"Everything okay, Hun?" his mom asked.

"Yeah, yeah, everything's okay," Timmy said, not wanting to tell her what he had done.

Once they arrived home, Timmy washed up to get ready for dinner and joined the rest of the family around the table for the not-so-typical taco Tuesday meal. Because Timmy's dad had to stay a little later at work and couldn't go to Timmy's game, he went straight home and was in charge of dinner. This meant the taco meat was a little browner than usual. But, with enough sour cream, no one could really tell.

After dinner, Mr. Taborsky pulled out his Bible and turned to Exodus 20 once again. "Tonight we're talking about commandment eight. It's in Exodus 20:15 and says,

'You shall not steal.'"

Timmy became wide-eyed and stared straight down at the table.

"What are some ways that we might steal?" asked Mr. Taborsky.

"Taking things from the store without paying!" Rose Marie jumped in, excited to know an answer.

"That's one way," Mrs. Taborsky said. "Any other ideas?"

Timmy remained silent, but Johnathon said, "Well, cheating in school or at work would be stealing as well, wouldn't it?"

"Definitely," Mr. Taborsky affirmed. "We can steal in many different ways. Wrongly taking answers from a test, a candy bar from a store, or a toy that doesn't belong to us are all ways people steal. Stealing is a big deal."

Rose Marie agreed by clapping her hands together with each syllable, "Yep! Yep! Yep!"

Mr. Taborsky continued, "But when someone steals, it has to do with what is going on in their heart. If someone feels the need to take something that isn't theirs, their heart and mind aren't remembering truth."

"What truth?" Johnathon asked.

"The truth that Jesus is enough and that no matter what we go through, we can be content in Him," Mr. Taborsky said. "There's a verse in Philippians 4:11 that shows us how the Apostle Paul lived this truth. Here it is:

> *'...for I have learned to be content whatever the circumstances. I know what it is to be in need, and I know what is to have plenty. I have learned the secret of being content in any and every situation, whether well fed or hungry, whether living in plenty or in want. I can do all this through him who gives me strength.'"*

"Many people misquote these verses. They think it means we can do anything we want because Jesus is on our side. But instead, Paul is saying no matter what he has or what he goes through, he is content because Christ is enough."

Mrs. Taborsky added, "We must always find contentment in Christ. I'm sure if Paul didn't, he would have wanted to steal food when he was hungry. Instead, he believed God would provide."

Timmy still sat in silence. He was sure his heart was beating loud enough for everyone else to hear.

Then finally, he burst out with, "I stole a piece of gum!" followed by a stream of tears.

"A piece of gum?" Johnathon said, asking as though he wasn't sure if gum was a cause for tears.

"What are you talking about, Timmy?" Mrs. Taborsky asked.

Timmy explained what happened, finishing with, "I even lied to you, Mom. You asked if I was okay earlier, and I really wasn't."

"Timmy, I'm glad you told us," Mr. Taborsky said, "and I'm glad you feel bad about it."

"You are?" asked Rose Marie.

"You are?" Timmy repeated the question through tear-filled eyes.

"Yes. God's Spirit lives in you, and He convicted you of something that God desires for you to repent of. God's Spirit guides us in ways to bring glory to Him. He helps us obey Him with our whole lives. When we disobey His leading, we often feel bad."

Timmy did feel better already, now that he had said what he did out loud.

"Let's talk more about this after dinner, Sweetie," Mrs. Taborsky said to Timmy.

Mr. Taborsky closed their family time in prayer, "God, thank you that we can look to You to provide all of our needs. We need Your forgiveness for not always finding all we need in Jesus, and we need Your Spirit to help us."

He paused and asked, "Timmy, do you want to pray out loud at all?"

Timmy felt nervous, "Sure... God, please forgive me for being disobedient and wrongly taking the piece of gum that wasn't mine. In Jesus' name, amen."

The Taborskys cleared the table and cleaned up from dinner.

A little later, Mrs. Taborsky sat with Timmy. Together they decided Timmy would need to figure out who he took the gum from and ask for forgiveness from them as well. This made him feel nervous too, but he knew it was the right thing.

At bedtime, Timmy crawled under his covers. He was not looking forward to admitting he was wrong to more people, but he wanted to obey God fully.

Closing his eyes to try to fall asleep, he prayed again, "God, thank You. Thank You for forgiving me, even when I choose to steal. Thank you for Jesus. Please help me to be more like Paul from the Bible. He seems to have known you so much that he could go through anything and not worry because he trusted You to provide. Help me to be like him."

Because he still felt nervous, it took Timmy a little longer to fall asleep that night. But after a little while, he finally drifted off to sleep.

Chapter 9

On this Tuesday morning in August, Timmy woke up a little earlier than normal, getting out of bed with the first hint of sunlight peeking through his window.

He was excited because today, his dad and brother were returning from their trip.

Every year, Mr. Taborsky took both of his sons on a trip. Timmy went somewhere with his dad in the winter. He always got to help decide what they would do, and each year it was different.

Johnathon's trip, on the other hand, was always in August, and he chose to do the same thing every year. He and his dad would travel a couple hours north to Bear Paw Lake for a fishing trip.

Johnathon has always loved the outdoors and has always loved to fish. At home, he would sleep in as late as possible, but on the fishing trip, he would get up before the sun so he could get as much fishing in as possible.

Timmy was so excited because Johnathon and his dad were getting back today. Sure he and Johnathon didn't always get along, but when he was gone, Timmy really did miss him. Plus, he was excited to hear all the great fishing stories!

Because Timmy was awake before both his mom or his sister, he quietly played with his toys on his bedroom floor.

When he heard the noise of his mom shuffling around to make coffee, he dashed out of his room.

"What time will Dad and Johnathon be home, Mom?" Timmy asked excitingly as he entered the kitchen.

"Well, good morning to you too, Timmy," Mrs. Taborsky said with a smile as she greeted Timmy with a kiss on top of his head. "I believe they should be home around ten o'clock."

It was only seven-thirty, and ten o'clock seemed like a long way off to Timmy.

Mrs. Taborsky must have known what Timmy was feeling, "After we eat breakfast, why don't you, Rose Marie, and I run and get some groceries before they get here? It will help the time go a little faster."

So, after breakfast, that's exactly what they did.

The trip to the store did help speed the time for Timmy. They pulled back in the driveway around 9:55am. They put the groceries away together and were then allowed to eat a pack of fruit snacks they had picked out at the store.

Timmy was biting into a blue raspberry flavored fruit snack when he heard the car door slam in the driveway—they were home!

Timmy and Rose Marie rushed to the back door to greet their dad and brother. "Welcome home!" they said together as the door opened.

"Hey, hey! There's my favorite four and seven-year-old!" Mr. Taborsky said, dropping some of his supplies at his feet so he could hug his greeters.

Johnathon was right behind him and received the same greeting with a big hug from both his brother and his sister.

"Hi, guys!" Johnathon said.

"How did it go? Did you catch any fish?" Timmy asked, excited to hear all about their four-day adventure.

"Oh, did we ever!" Johnathon replied with a big smile, "Follow me, and I'll tell you about it."

Timmy and Rose Marie followed Johnathon into his bedroom. There Johnathon filled them in on the long weekend.

He retold much of what happened, giving them all the details he could remember of each fish he caught.

"But then," he said a little way into his stories, "on Monday morning, you wouldn't believe what happened!"

"What? What?!" Rose Marie asked in excitement.

"Well, I knew something was different because my pole almost jerked out of my hand," Johnathon continued, "and that was just the beginning of what must have been an hour fight to get this fish reeled in!"

"An hour?!" Timmy asked.

"It must've been!" Johnathon exclaimed. "And when I finally got it to the dock, there it was, the largest fish I had ever seen! I mean, it was this big," Johnathon said while stretching his arms apart as far as they could go.

"Woah!" Timmy said as he and Rose Marie stood there wide-eyed at their brother's story.

"Kids! It's time for lunch!" Mrs. Taborsky yelled from the kitchen.

They ran to wash their hands and then joined their mom and dad at the table. It was rare that they all ate lunch together during the week because Mr. Taborsky was usually at work. But since he was home, they sat down together.

They enjoyed sandwiches, and Johnathon continued to share more details from the trip.

Once they were finished eating, Mr. Taborsky said, "Why don't we do our family devotions now since we're all together."

He left to get his Bible. Returning, he said, "We're in Exodus 20:16 now. This is the ninth commandment:

> *'You shall not give false testimony against your neighbor.'"*

Mr. Taborsky explained, "A lot of times we hear this commandment simplified to 'Don't lie.' In the Old Testament, it was specifically a command to not lie about what someone did or didn't do. Lying about those things in that culture could be the difference between life or death."

"Lying can lead to death?" Rose Marie asked wide-eyed and worried.

"Our culture is different now, Sweetie," Mrs. Taborsky said. "We don't punish people with death if they lie. But, all sin does separate us from God. And if we do not repent from sin and believe in Jesus Christ as Lord and Savior of our lives, we are spiritually dead."

"Yes," Mr. Taborsky agreed. "And remember, when Jesus is our Lord, he holds us to a very high standard with the way we use our words. If we claim to follow Him, we are expected to speak only truth. We aren't to lie about what *others* do or don't do. But we are also not to lie about what *we* ourselves do, no matter how big or small it seems to us."

He finished by saying, "We need to realize that all of our words are a reflection of the One we claim to serve. The Bible tells us what comes out of our mouths is a reflection of our heart. So we need to always ask God to make sure that our hearts are all about Him and not ourselves."

The Taborskys bowed their heads to pray.

"Wait!" Johnathon interrupted, "I need to say something."

They all looked up towards him, still holding hands.

"Rose Marie and Timmy, I wasn't completely honest with you earlier when I was telling you my fishing stories. I mean, I *did* fight with a fish for the longest I ever had. And I *do* believe it was the biggest fish I had ever caught... but I didn't fight with it for an hour, and it was probably only about this big," Johnathon spread his hands apart about a third of the distance then what he had earlier. "I'm sorry. I guess I just wanted it to be even more exciting to hear about than it already was, but that wasn't right."

"I forgive you," Timmy said.

"Oh me too!" Rose Marie agreed.

"Thanks, guys," Johnathon responded.

"Would you like to close our time in prayer?" Mr. Taborsky asked Johnathon.

"Sure," Johnathon said, bowing his head. "Thank You, God, for the fishing trip and all the fish that Dad and I got to catch. Please forgive me for not always being completely truthful. Sorry for using words to make me look better instead of You. Please help all of us to be different in the world so that others can know You through the way we act and speak. In Jesus' name, amen."

The Taborsky clan cleaned up from lunch and enjoyed the rest of the afternoon outside together.

Timmy and Johnathon played catch in the yard. While they were throwing the ball to each other, Timmy couldn't help but think how cool his big brother was.

Obeying God and being honest is way cooler than any fish story ever could be, he thought, throwing the ball to Johnathon.

Timmy caught the ball again.

God, help me to be truthful so that others can know you more with my life! He prayed in his heart.

He threw the ball back to Johnathon, this time with all of his might.

Chapter 10

E veryone is starting to feel the freedom of summer slowly fade away. But before school stole summer away completely, there are still a few things the Taborskys had planned.

One of those things for Timmy is Colin's birthday party.

Colin was one of Timmy's friends. He wasn't Timmy's best friend, that was Bryce, but Colin was still a good friend. They are both on the Spice Lake Salamanders team this summer and have been on the same tee-ball team the past two summers.

Colin has a birthday party every year, and they are always very cool. There is a theme with awesome decorations, the best food, and unbelievably fun games.

The party is always at his house, which is in the really nice part of Spice Lake. There the houses are double the size of the Taborkys' house. Colin's family even has a pool in their backyard!

Timmy was excited to see what Colin had planned for his party this year.

After lunch, Timmy, with the help of his mom, put together the present they had gotten for Colin. It was a cool building block set of a pirate ship. The set even had a parrot that sat on the shoulder of the pirate!

Around two o'clock, Timmy and Mrs. Taborsky got in the car and drove over to Colin's house. As they pulled up, it was clear what this year's theme was: dinosaurs!

They got out of the car and were greeted by a T-Rex.

"Welcome!" the T-Rex said.

Once it spoke, Timmy knew that the T-Rex was Colin's dad dressed in one of those inflatable costumes.

"Timmy, why don't you head in the backyard. Estelle, the other ladies are just inside," the dinosaur said, ending with a roar.

Mrs. Taborsky said goodbye to Timmy, heading towards the front door. The moms always hung out together during Colin's party and had a mini-party of their own.

Timmy walked in the backyard. Going through the gate, he felt like he was stepping through some sort of time machine. There, before his very own eyes, was a land of years past.

The water slide for the pool had been transformed to look like a volcano with red lava pouring out of it. Timmy noticed that kids were climbing up the back of it and sliding down the red lava into the pool!

Timmy spotted Bryce in a huge sandbox on the other side of the yard. He dropped his present for Colin off at the gift table and ran to meet him.

"Hi, Timmy! Grab a brush and help me discover dinosaur bones!" Bryce said. He was already working with a couple other kids to excavate dinosaur bones that were buried underneath the sand.

Timmy grabbed a brush and jumped right in!

After they had uncovered a dinosaur fossil, they swam for a little bit. Then they played this new type of tag Colin called

'Dinosaur Tag' where everyone had to tuck their arms in their sleeves and run around with short T-Rex arms.

Later they watched Colin open presents and ate cake. The cake was no ordinary cake. Everyone got their own little one to eat, and it was shaped like a small volcano with chocolate lava oozing out of it, and in the very center, there was a hidden dinosaur toy that everyone got to keep.

The party was a blast, and it went by really fast. Timmy was sad when it was over.

After saying goodbye to Colin, Bryce, and the T-Rex, Timmy got back in the car with his mom.

"So, how was the party for you?" Mrs. Taborsky asked.

"Oh, it was sooooo cool, Mom!" Timmy exclaimed. He told her all the things that they did as quickly as he could, trying not to leave anything out.

"That's great, Sweetie. Colin's family really knows how to put on a great party, don't they?" Mrs. Taborsky said.

Timmy thought she sounded a little sad when she spoke, "Did *you* have a good time, mom?"

"Of course. Sherry always does a great job of hosting," she responded. Then she quickly changed the subject by asking, "Did Colin like his building block set?"

"He loved it!" Timmy gave two thumbs up to his mom from the backseat.

Once they got home, Timmy rushed to show Rose Marie his dinosaur toy while Mrs. Taborsky rushed to find Mr. Taborsky.

After Timmy filled in Rose Marie with all that he did at the party, he went to the kitchen to get some water. There, his mom and dad were having a discussion.

Mrs. Taborsky was explaining the new remodel that Colin's

parents had just done on their kitchen, "Honey, it was *really* nice. I just loved it!"

Mr. Taborsky stood quietly while Mrs. Taborsky went on, "You know I've been thinking about updating our kitchen. If we do the work ourselves, I'm sure it would be a fraction of what they paid. Plus, our kitchen is much smaller than theirs, so it would definitely be cheaper!"

"Hmmm," Mr. Taborsky said thoughtfully. "If this is really something that you want, why don't you do a little research and we'll see if we can make it work."

Timmy could hear the excitement in his mom's voice but didn't think much of the conversation.

The next couple of days were pretty normal. The only difference Timmy noticed was that his mom was on the internet a little more than usual. She was looking at different kitchen cabinet styles, looking up instructions on how to tile, and comparing different paint colors.

———◆———

It was now Tuesday night.

Just like always, the Taborskys had their typical taco Tuesday meal, and Mr. Taborsky pulled out His Bible.

"Can you believe it? Tonight is the final commandment," he said right before reading Exodus 20:17:

> *"'You shall not covet your neighbor's house. You shall not covet your neighbor's wife, or his male or female servant, his ox or donkey, or anything that belongs to your neighbor.'"*

"Hmmm, does anyone know what 'covet' means?" Mr. Taborsky asked.

"Doesn't it mean wanting? Like wanting your neighbor's house, or wanting your neighbor's wife?" Johnathon asked.

"That's right," Mr. Taborsky affirmed. "Coveting is something that happens internally, or inside our hearts and minds. It has to do with what we want or desire. The opposite of coveting is contentment."

"So, I can't want anything?" Rose Marie asked.

Mr. Taborsky responded, "It isn't bad to want nice things, but when we covet things in our hearts, we aren't *just* wanting nice things. When we covet, we are forgetting to depend on Jesus. When we forget that all we need is found in Him, it leads to other sins like stealing, dishonesty, or even idolatry."

"Oh my!" Mrs. Taborksy said with a big sigh. "Isn't this perfectly fitting for me! I have definitely been wrong by coveting this week."

"What do you mean, Mommy?" Rose Marie looked up at her mom with her big eyes.

She went on to confess, "I have been coveting Colin's family's kitchen. My want for a kitchen like theirs took over my thoughts, time, and energy the past couple days, and I quickly became discontent with the nice kitchen I already have."

Looking over at Timmy, she said, "Actually, I should have learned a lesson from Timmy."

Timmy was shocked, *I taught Mom something?* he thought.

His shock was noticed by Mrs. Taborsky, who smiled at him, "Timmy, you didn't once complain after Colin's party about not having something that you experienced there. Instead, you were excited and thankful for what you did get to experience. I should have allowed the Holy Spirit to teach me by your example."

Timmy was surprised. He hadn't really thought about the way he acted after the party.

The Taborskys finished their devotions, this time with Mrs. Taborsky praying, "Dear Heavenly Father, thank You for Your truth. Thank you for Your Holy Spirit who shows truth to us in a loving, personal way. Please forgive me for coveting in my heart and for comparing my kitchen to Sherry's. Please help all of us to find true contentment in You and in Your Son, Jesus. In His name, we come to you, amen."

Timmy laid in bed that night thinking about what his mom had said, *How could I teach my mom a lesson?* he thought.

He remembered a song that they sang in Sunday school a lot. It was a verse song from 1 Timothy 4:12 and started with the lyrics: *"Don't let anyone look down on you because you are young, but set an example for the believers..."*

Timmy was so thankful that God could use him, a seven-year-old, to help others follow Him better.

With that song running through his head, Timmy drifted off to sleep.

Chapter 11

S ummer is ending in Spice Lake, and everyone is preparing to return to school.

With the end of summer, there is great excitement to reconnect with friends, but also great sadness. Each kid has to say goodbye to the things that make summer so great. Bare feet, bike rides, cannonballs in the pool, and ice cream cones are all left behind once school arrives.

For Timmy, he is sad that the Spice Lake Salamanders' season has finished. They had a great season with ten wins and only two losses. It really was a great first baseball season. He, along with Bryce, Glenn, and Colin were already planning to be on the same team again next summer.

But, the planning for next summer had to be paused because planning for the school year was now the main focus.

To get ready for school, every family in Spice Lake receives a supplies list. These lists are given by each teacher. Whatever they decide students need in their classroom, they put on a list for their families to buy.

These lists are available pretty early on in the summer. But, in the typical Taborsky way, Mrs. Taborsky, along with Rose Marie, Timmy, and Johnathon, were out the day before school started to search for the items on their lists.

As they arrived at the store, Mrs. Taborsky put the van in park and then looked at her children as though she was a coach of a football team entering the final quarter, "Alright! You guys know the drill. We go straight for the school supplies, we find what we need, we mark it off, and we move on. Last year it took us sixty-two minutes. Let's see if we can shave some time off this year! If we can, we may just have time for some ice cream!"

Mrs. Taborsky always knew how to motivate the Taborsky children.

They all unbuckled, and like a pack of wolves on a hunt, they were laser-focused and headed straight for the school supply section.

Because they had waited so long, the school supply section had clearly been picked over. There were still plenty of options, but they weren't all in the right spot, and if you wanted a certain color or style, it was going to require some digging.

The disorganized aisles didn't throw the Taborskys for a loop. They were ready to get things done.

Mrs. Taborsky handed Johnathon his list, "You're in charge of your list this year, Johnathon," she said. "Let me know if you need help."

She then took Rose Marie and Timmy and started helping them go through their lists.

She sent Timmy to find folders for his class. He needed three, so he dug through the pile and found two gold right away. After a little more searching, he found a blue one. Of course, he had to find the two colors of the Spice Lake Salamanders!

Every time Timmy returned to the cart, Mrs. Taborsky

would give him another item to find and bring back. They had a pretty smooth system.

Rose Marie, on the other hand, was a little overwhelmed. It was her first year getting ready for PreK, and she could not decide which backpack she wanted. She kept going between *Cordelia, the Candy Queen,* which had a sparkly lollipop design, and *Chica Cheetah* that had the catchphrase, "Aprendamos!" written in cheetah print letters across the back.

After changing her mind no less than six times, Rose Marie finally selected the *Chica Cheetah* bag.

Johnathon returned from the other aisle that had more "grown-up" supplies as Timmy was grabbing his last item: a box of crayons. He was extra excited about this box because it had the special crayon sharpener built into the box!

"We're making good time! We're at forty minutes crew," Mrs. Taborsky said. "But we still have to get through checkout."

Mrs. Taborsky, Timmy, and Rose Marie rushed to the checkout line while Johnathon was sent to grab milk and then meet them upfront.

Timmy was in charge of choosing the line he thought would be the fastest. He chose line #3, mostly because three is his favorite number.

Johnathon met them with plenty of time before they piled their items on the belt and went through the checkout process.

Once the items were purchased, they all grabbed bags and rushed to the car, put the bags in the trunk, and hurried to buckle.

Mrs. Taborsky looked at her phone, "Fifty-three minutes! Way to go! That's almost ten minutes off our time last year."

The Taborsky kids high-fived each other, and Rose Marie let out a squeal, "Ice creeeeeaaaaammmmm!"

As they drove to get ice cream, Rose Marie continued to talk. "Mommy, how many things did we get for *me*?"

"Hmmm, well, we got your backpack, your nap mat, your lunch box... do you remember what else?"

"Hmmmmmmmmmm, pencils and crayons!" Rose Marie remembered out loud.

"That's right, pencils and crayons, and a pencil box to put them in." Mrs. Taborsky added.

"I grabbed tissues and hand sanitizer for you, remember?" Timmy said.

"That's right, and then we had to get a pair of scissors and one more thing. Do you remember, Rose Marie?" Mrs. Taborsky asked.

"Oh yeah, my gluuue stiiiicck!" Rose Marie said as she sang and did a little dance, always finding a way to add a little flair to every conversation.

"That makes ten items, was that how many things were on her list, Mom?" Timmy asked.

"I believe so!" Mrs. Taborsky said.

"Ten?! That's just like the Ten Commandments!" Rose Marie exclaimed. She was proud of herself for remembering something from family devotion time.

She continued, "Aaaand, just like my school list, I'm gonna mark off the Ten Commandments list as I get them done!"

"Well, Sweetie, the Ten Commandments is a type of list; you're right about that. But it isn't the same kind of list as your school supply list," Mrs. Taborsky said.

"What do you mean, Mommy?" Rose Marie asked.

"Well, we don't mark off the Ten Commandments once

they are completed. It's something that we need to look back at every day—well every moment really," Mrs. Taborsky said.

"Ugggggh!" Rose Marie said dramatically. "You mean we never get to complete the Ten Commandments list?"

Timmy first thought his sister's questions were funny, but then he began to feel that same "ugggh!" feeling inside. It seemed very overwhelming to always have to look at the Ten Commandments. Living your life by these lists of rules and knowing that you can never cross them off did not sound fun.

Johnathon piped in at this point, "Mom, doesn't Dad always say that these rules were given by God for our good?"

"That's right. We won't ever be able to keep God's list perfectly..."

"Then why do we try again?" Timmy blurted out.

"Well, God gave us these rules because we were created *by* Him *for* Him. His guidelines help us live the way we were made to live. Our sin and selfishness get in the way of living this way, but in God's great love and grace, He has provided Jesus and His Spirit. Jesus' perfect life covers our mistakes, and His Spirit guides us to change and follow Him more closely."

By this time, Mrs. Taborsky had pulled into Sophie's Ice Cream Parlor and parked. She turned to face her children in the backseat and continued, "We went into the store today to get our list done and over with, but our attitude towards God's list is much different. When we know God more, we see His heart and how good, holy, and loving He is. Our response to who He is and how He treats us is to follow Him as close as we can. This means loving Him and others."

"Great!" Rose Marie said as she unbuckled herself. It was

clear she knew where they were. She had stopped listening once she saw the light-up ice cream cone that sits in the window of the ice cream store.

But, Timmy was listening and soaking up everything that his mom said.

That night, as the Taborsky kids were getting ready for bed, Mr. Taborsky told them to come to the living room once they were done brushing their teeth.

Once they were all gathered, Mr. Taborsky said, "I want to pray as a family to give this school year to the Lord."

Timmy was still thinking about the conversation they had earlier in the van, "Can I pray, Dad?" he asked.

"Of course!" Mr. Taborsky said with a big grin.

Timmy bowed his head, "Dear God, thank You for Your list, the Ten Commandments. Thank You for giving us rules to live by—not to make our life harder, but better. Thank You for giving us Jesus to live perfectly and cover our mistakes, and thank You for Your Spirit. I ask that You help each of us this school year follow You closer. In Jesus' name, amen."

Each member of the Taborsky family agreed with Timmy's prayer, "Amen."

After Timmy said goodnight to his brother and sister, his mom and dad tucked him in bed.

Timmy laid there thinking about all the great things he got to do this summer. He couldn't believe how fast it went and how much fun he had.

He remembered the Taborsky Tuesday devotionals and all that he learned. God really changed his heart this summer. With each commandment they talked about, he realized his need for Jesus more.

Closing his eyes, Timmy was excited about the first day of third grade the next day. He was excited to depend on God's Spirit to help him love God and others, especially the other kids in his class.

Turning to his side and pulling his covers tight to his chin, Timmy drifted off to sleep for the final night of his summer adventure.

Made in the USA
Monee, IL
11 December 2019